Mealtime

First Aladdin Books edition 1990
Text copyright © 1983, 1988 by Walker Books Ltd
Illustrations copyright © 1988 by Maureen Roffey

Aladdin Books
Macmillan Publishing Company
866 Third Avenue, New York, NY 10022
Printed in Hong Kong

A hardcover edition of *Mealtime* is available from
Four Winds Press, Macmillan Publishing Company.
10 9 8 7 6 5 4 3 2 1

Library of Congress Cataloging-in-Publication Data

Roffey, Maureen.
Mealtime/Maureen Roffey. — 1st Aladdin Books ed. p.   cm.
Summary: Pictures and questions stimulate the reader to
talk about food and eating.
ISBN 0-689-70809-2
[1. Eating customs — Fiction. 2. Food — Fiction.] I. Title.
[PZ7.R6255Me   1990] [E] — dc20
89-48006 CIP AC

Mealtime

Maureen Roffey

Aladdin Books
Macmillan Publishing Company
New York

Playing leapfrog makes you hungry.
Skipping makes you hungry too.

What else makes you hungry?

Who else gets hungry?
What do all these animals eat?

When your tummy rumbles
it is time to eat.
Wash your hands first.

Then help set the table.

What things go on the table?

Now for the food.
Here is a bowl of soup.
What soup do you like best?

Here is a plate of vegetables.
What is your favorite vegetable?

This is pasta.

How do you eat pasta?

Not with your hands!

What do you hold in your hands to eat?

There are lots of different kinds of
fruits and vegetables.

Can you name all these?
What color are they?

There are lots of different drinks.

milk for the baby

orange juice　　　　lemonade

tea for Mom and coffee for Dad
What drinks do you like?

What do you eat and drink for a picnic?
Do you like picnics?

What special occasion is this?
What else happens at parties?

What do you do when you have finished eating?

Where do all the pots and pans belong?

Mealtime is over – time for a walk.
Ready, set, go!

MELON

ORANGE

PEAR

PINEAPPLE

CHERRIES

GRAPES

BANANAS

APPLE

STRAWBERRY

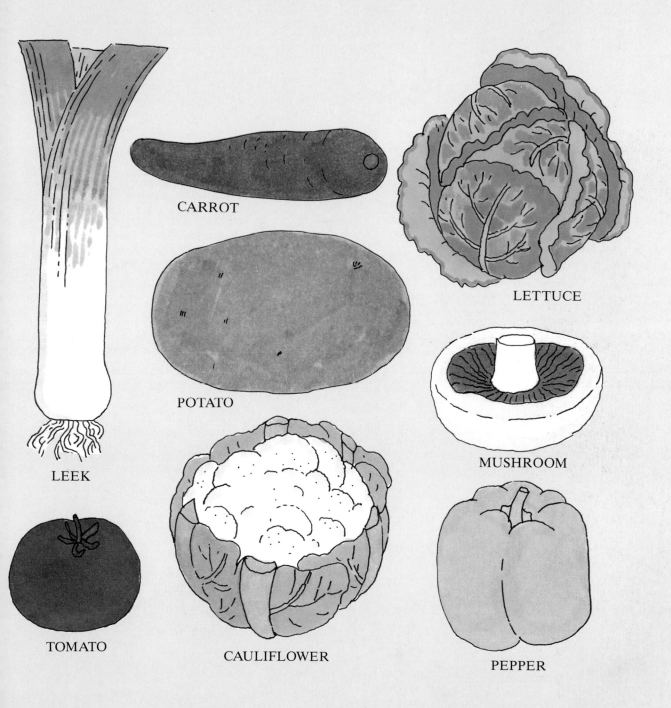

CARROT

LETTUCE

POTATO

MUSHROOM

LEEK

TOMATO

CAULIFLOWER

PEPPER